Why Am I an

Jane Annunziata, PsyD
Marc A. Nemiroff, PhD

Illustrated by Margaret Scott

Magination Press • Washington, DC

Published by
MAGINATION PRESS
An Educational Publishing Foundation Book
American Psychological Association
750 First Street, NE
Washington, DC 20002

Illustrated by Margaret Scott, Washington, DC
Typeset in Cheltenham and printed by Worzalla Publishing, Stevens Point, WI
Production coordinated by Valerie Montenegro

Library of Congress Cataloging-in-Publication Data
Annunziata, Jane.
    Why am I an only child? / Jane Annunziata, Marc A. Nemiroff;
  illustrated by Margaret Scott.
        p.   cm.
    Summary: Because Eudora, a little rhino, is an only child, she
tries to talk her parents into giving her a brother or sister so
that she will no longer be lonely.
    ISBN 1-55798-506-5 (acid-free paper)
    [1. Only child—Fiction. 2. Parent and child—Fiction.
3. Emotions—Fiction. 4. Rhinoceroses—Fiction.]   I. Nemiroff, Marc A.   II.
Scott, Margaret,
  ill. III. Title.
PZ7.A5876Wh   1998
{E}—DC21   98-13858
                                                              CIP
                                                               AC

Manufactured in the United States of America
10 9 8 7 6 5 4 3 2 1

For Bret and Gabriel,
our own very special only children,
with love

Eudora wants a brother...

or a

Sister...

PATRICK'S BROTHER

PATRICK

Patrick has a brother.

Molly has a sister.

Eudora thought and thought.

Eudora was confused.

She felt different from her friends.

Sometimes she was

too.

Why am I an Only CHILD?

Don't you want MORE like ME?

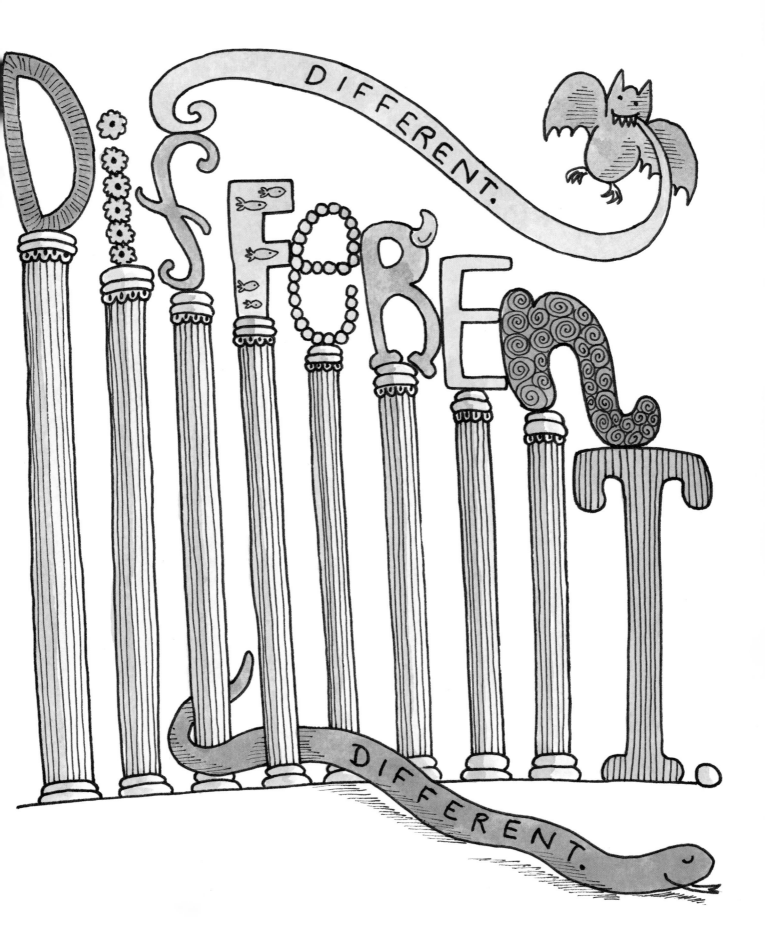

Some families are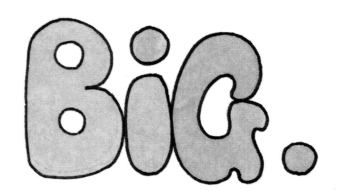

Some families are small.
There are all kinds of families.
That's what makes the world

Interesting for you, but not for me!

I want to be the boss of this.

And even if I don't have a brother or sister, I DO have friends and cousins and neighbors.

EVERY FAMILY
HAS ITS OWN
RIGHT
SIZE.

NOTE TO PARENTS AND GUARDIANS

There are many children in the United States who live in single-child families. Our experience as child psychologists has helped us appreciate that only children can feel different, lonely, and confused about why they do not have brothers or sisters as so many of their age-mates do. Parents of only children are sometimes uncertain about how to help their child with these feelings and answer the often inevitable question: "Why don't I have a brother or sister?" Parents of only children want to ensure that their child does not feel shortchanged and that their only child knows that he or she is very loved. Our book is intended to help only children understand that families come in different sizes and that every family needs to find *its own* right size.

This story describes the variety of feelings that an only child might have, including anger, sadness, or confusion about why her parents do not have more children. In this story, our little rhinoceros, Eudora, is helped to express, understand, and resolve her feelings about being an only child. She starts out confused and upset about not having a brother or sister and, by the end of the book, feels content because she understands that families come in different sizes and that there are actually good things about being an only child.

This book is written for young children 4 to 7 years old. As parents read this book to their children, they can encourage discussion of their own child's feelings and reactions as compared with Eudora's. We hope that Eudora will help parents understand their child's feelings, and help only children feel positive about living in a single-child family.

Jane Annunziata and Marc A. Nemiroff